# HAUNTED DESIRES

**From USA Today Bestselling Authors Willow Winters & Amelia Wilde comes a spicy short, perfect for spooky season.**

At first, it was a crush — then it was a spell.

He's tall, handsome, and mysterious... and the librarian for the ancient texts. Basically, a witch's dream.

Cue Hazel, the owner of a charming little shop on Main Street called Bewitched Boutique. In need of town records, she finds herself visiting the library more often, sharing stolen glances with the object of her growing affection.

When Hazel's crush turns into a burning need to kiss Finley, she decides a spell is in order.

Little does she know, Finley's past comes with haunted desires of its own.

# HAZEL

If you want to become a witch, the first thing you must do is learn your soul's history.

That means tracing your family tree and finding out what kind of woman your mother was, and your grandmother, and *her* grandmother. That means researching as much as you can about your *father's* grandmother, and *her* grandmother, and every other woman you can discover until you lose the trail.

At least that's what the last book I read told me. Why? Because magic comes from the marrow of our bones, and witches pass those sparks of magic waiting to be ignited down to their daughters, and it changes along the way, adapting, surviving, and waiting...especially if one of those women tried to fight her true nature and forget about magic and spirits entirely.

I think every girl goes through a Salem witch trials phase. I went through mine in middle school, which is when I started to look into any possible witchy history my family had, and I found a lot more than I expected. The delight is still as nerve-racking as it is thrilling. That small moment in time before denial settled in.

It didn't seem real to me then—I was too young to understand the true power of spells and intentions and history—so once that phase burned out, I left it behind. I lived my life and finished school and went off to college. A business degree seemed practical. A minor in botany and herbalism is less so, but I was drawn to it.

That was where history found me again.

Cedar Lane kept popping up in all my research projects. Even my hobbies somehow found a way to be related. It was like the world was pushing me back to the path my ancestors had forged for me. Maybe even to bring me back to where I started—a full circle kind of thing.

So when I heard through a friend that Merideth, an older woman with thin-rimmed spectacles and wrinkles around her eyes that showed her age, wanted someone to take over her little shop on Main Street, I knew it wasn't a coincidence. Cedar Lane was calling me home. Complete with a witchy shop of candles, crystals, books, and a backroom of *curiosities*. And of course a little corner with tea and coffee and pastries from the corner bakery. After all, Merideth always had time for tea and tea leaf readings.

Now Bewitched Boutique is all mine. Plants crowd the windowsill. Rosemary, mint, thyme, and basil along with a beautiful pothos that climbs the bookshelf. With a little bell that dings every so often, lifting my eyes from my family heritage to the rainy outdoors of Main Street. The narrow storefront is like a second home to me, and I've tried to make it into a second home for anyone who wanders in. I keep an electric kettle on hand for people who like tea and a pot of coffee on hand complete with all the syrups. Although I can't offer a reading, I am not attuned in those ways. I keep Merideth's bell chimes by the door for protection. And I do my best to keep anything a local witch might need in stock, too. I'm constantly accepting deliveries of dried herbs and crystals and tarot cards. Lavender and sage are popular. Not as popular as black salt though, a necessity for protection. Oddly enough, rose bath bombs for Aphrodite baths and yellow candles to light for success can hardly stay on the shelves. It's interesting what I pick up on the person across the register while I ring in their order. I always keep their secrets though. Especially those who come in with desperation and have questions. I've learned much in the years of my studies.

Some people in town think my shop is a joke. Some people think I'm running it out of kindness or because I owed Merideth something. Some people think I want to make a profit off the occult history in the area.

As I close up shop for the day, I know the truth is different.

I run this shop—*my* shop—because it connects me to something deeper inside that I can't place. It lets me feel the changes in Cedar Lane as the seasons pass and stand in the places my great-grandmothers walked before me.

Most of all, it lets me live close to the library. And with that thought, the clock turns to eight at night.

Locking the door, I readjust my bag on my shoulder, pull my hood over my head, and make my way toward the library. My heart skips a beat as I go. My breath fogs in front of my face from the chilly fall night air.

It's three blocks down and two blocks back from Main Street, and it's one of the oldest buildings in town. My boots click on the pavement as I go. The roads are vacant this time of night. The soft patter of the light rain accompanies the clicking. The library started life as the town hall over a hundred and sixty years ago, then became the courthouse, and finally became the library when they built a new courthouse on the other side of town.

The sun starts to set as I turn onto the sidewalk leading to the library. There are two lights out front on either side of the old large door, and they *click* on as I get closer, lighting the limestone steps. The former courthouse and town hall is made of more limestone with a peaked roof in the middle and a peak on either side. A shiver runs through me as I hurry up the steps. I love an old, imposing building, and it's even more imposing when the nights are longer.

For a second or two, I imagine coming here for a trial or a tense town meeting. I can almost hear the voices murmuring inside and the arguments starting to boil over.

But then I pull open the heavy wooden door, and it's only the quiet library. It's the last hour of the day. It closes at nine so it's typically quiet this hour.

With only a few patrons or no one but the librarian...Finley.

With his dark eyes cast down reading the book in his hands, he stands behind the circulation desk in the middle of what used to be the main hall of the courthouse. It's the main room of the library now, and most of the space is taken with packed shelves.

I inhale the scent of old polished floors and old books and even older stone, and the librarian glances over at me.

It doesn't sound like anyone else is here, but I offer a wave to him instead of a verbal greeting just in case and use the moment as an excuse to look at him. To admire him even.

Finley is tall and dark haired and as quiet as the library itself. There's an air of mystery and power that clings to him. There are secrets in his dark eyes, and I've wanted to know what they are since I moved back here after college. He's fit and broad shouldered, and I often wondered how his chest would feel. How his full lips would taste on mine.

And I've tried—God, I'm embarrassed to admit this—I've tried to flirt with this man more times than I can count. I've asked him questions about the notebooks he's always writing in. I've asked him his opinion about the historical books I spend most of my time poring over. I know he's enjoyed similar books on herbalism.

I've tried and tried to get him to let me in, and he doesn't seem to pick up on the fact that I'm... interested.

*Very* interested.

Tall, secretive men with dark hair are my type, and I haven't met many men who frequent the same sections of the library as I do and who have an air around them like...

Like it's magic. I'm drawn to him in ways I cannot explain. He feels like shadowy, illicit magic. Like he knows more than his own secrets. Like he might know secrets about the library and the town, and possibly even me.

A burst of laughter echoes out of one of the side rooms, interrupting my thoughts. The library isn't empty after all. I sweep my hood off my hair and make a beeline for the very back, which is where the oldest books are kept. The ones you have to have permission to open.

I put my bag and coat at my usual table at the end of the row, then take out the little notebook I've been carrying with me for years and page through it, my heart pounding. I barely see the notes I've written on the most recent pages. I'm far too busy with wondering what it is he's reading.

This is getting me nowhere. I close the notebook, close my eyes, and breathe.

I can smell his cologne.

It's faint, as if Finley walked through this aisle a minute or two ago, and yet it's totally distinct from the woodsy smell of the shelves and the old-paper scent of the books.

Oh, God, I cannot be smelling his cologne right now.

But it's *good*. It's subtle and historical, like the library, but there's an element to it that I can't name. It reminds me a little of my shop, but what?

I inhale again but still can't name it.

Okay. That's enough. I can handle being in the library with Finley, and I can handle what I came here to do, which is research on all the town's most infamous families.

The most powerful magic comes from working together, and not all of that magic has to do with spell-casting or glimpsing the future. Sometimes, it has to do with the bonds we form from being in a community together. Helping one another in times of need or just times of togetherness.

That's what covens are for. Companionship and togetherness are their own form of rituals.

I came across a small box of letters shortly after I moved back that hinted at the existence of a coven in a town over in the late 1700s. After I got settled in, I started to explore its existence more deeply and found strong ties between many of the families in that town. The wealthier families left *more* records, but that doesn't mean they're the only ones. There are mentions of the other members if you know where to look.

For example, most families—wealthy or not—kept some kind of record of their business dealings, and you can find all sorts of clues in those ledgers. A bundle of garden plants sold here, a silver spoon sold there. A deal made between two families, one supplying glass and one supplying silver to make a perfectly circular mirror. Sometimes, if you're very lucky, someone will have made a note about a deal being made at a weekly meeting and listed the names of the women in attendance.

I open my notebook again. I have a rough sketch of the town as it used to be in the seventeen and eighteen hundreds—scans of the real documents are on my computer—and a list of names I want to research on the opposite page. I read over them one more time, then get to work.

The laughter in the rest of the library fades away. I barely notice Finley's voice as he speaks to someone at the circulation desk. Although, I do notice. I take down one old volume after another, bring them to the table, and go through them page by page.

At some point, the front door of the library closes with a loud *bang*, and a new silence settles over the stacks. A whisper of cold air brushes the back of my neck, but I don't pay attention. It must be a draft from the front door.

I'm almost finished with another volume when I inhale more cologne.

Finley is on the other side of the narrow aisle, reshelving some books. He scans each shelf slowly, carefully, his eyes landing on every spine as he goes past.

He's still there when I get to the last page in the volume and close it as quietly as I can.

And then...

I have to go over there.

Because he's standing at the shelf where this book goes.

Finley glances at me as I approach, his dark eyes

flickering up and down my body. Heat floods my body and there's a little flip in the pit of my stomach. He gives me a terse, professional nod.

I nod back at him, ignoring the blush rising in my cheeks.

The gap where my book belongs is right in front of him.

I swallow thickly, suddenly unable to function normally. "Excuse me," I murmur, and step closer. It's a thick book, so it's heavy, and I need both hands to lift it back to its place.

He's so close.

There are only inches between the books in his hands and my back. Only inches between the heat of his body and mine. He's holding his breath.

I lift the book, and then his hand is over mine, helping me push it onto the shelf.

"Thank you," I say, and take a quick step to the side. We're still *so close* in the aisle. "I was also looking for..."

My face is so hot that it's hard to see the call numbers on the spines of the books. I have to pull out my notebook to double-check it, and—

It's on the shelf right in front of Finley. A little farther down than the book I just put back.

"I was looking for..." I point. "It's that red one, if you could..."

He grabs the book off the shelf and passes it to me. Our fingers brush together on the old leather, and I feel the heat of that touch all up my arm. A quiet gasp comes from somewhere nearby, like an echo. Did *I* do that? Or was it someone else?

*Thump, thump, thump,* my heart pounds.

Finley hasn't broken contact. I don't pull my hand away. He just stops and waits, and I stop, too, finally managing to look up into his dark eyes.

They're *very* dark. The red in his cheeks is pretty dark, too. I'm almost transfixed by it. Like *he's* the one who's been calling to me. He's the one I should've been researching. He's the one I should be studying.

I *am* studying him. I can't tear my eyes away. I start to go up on tiptoe, drawn in by the electric tension between us, and he takes a short breath, tipping his head down—

The front door of the library opens, letting in another gust of wind. "Finley?" a voice calls. "Oh, I'm freezing to death. Finley, where are you? I'm here about that hold I placed. It's here, isn't it?"

Clearing his throat and straightening his shoulders, Finley pulls away, turning toward the footsteps coming toward the back of the library.

"There are other volumes in the back," he says quickly and quietly before he leaves. "They're only available by appointment."

"Oh?" I say breathlessly. "When could—"

"Tomorrow night, once the library's closed."

"Yes," I agree without taking a breath. *Thump, thump, thump,* my heart races.

He gives me one more nod, and then he's gone. Leaving me in more suspense than I've been in since I first came back home to that shop.

## 2

## HAZEL

Not a darn thing productive gets done for the rest of the evening. My research is stagnant as my thoughts are concerned with something else. Or rather, *someone* else.

How am I supposed to think when I just had an encounter like that with Finley? He's never stood close enough to touch before. He's *never* come to the back of the library by the local history section when I'm back there.

Our fingers have never touched before.

The touch still lingers.

And the way he looked at me, up and down, his eyes going dark... It was just the two of us. The tension cracked, and I swear there was something there. He must feel what I feel. I know it to be so.

The way he held his breath, like he wanted to touch me but couldn't bring himself to...

I leave the library well before closing and skirt the outside of the stacks. If I see him again, I'll say something awkward, and I just don't want the spell to break. It was too real. Too obvious.

It occurs to me on the walk home that a *spell* might be exactly what's needed. My lips twitch up with hope, a *spell* will do nicely.

It's a blustery night, cool and clear, and as I take in the fresh air, I can't help but notice the energy all around me. It's electric and powerful. The moon is the smallest sliver of a crescent. So close to the new moon.

It's impossible to think about anything else when I can still feel the place where Finley's fingers touched mine. It's like I've veered off the path I was on and onto an unfamiliar one.

My apartment couldn't be more familiar. More like a refuge for my racing thoughts. I live in a cute two-story apartment building with eight units. Mine is the one closest to the trees on the opposite side of the lot, which means it's also closest to the river that runs through the woods. The backyard is nothing but trees and a few potted plants on my concrete patio. That's a good thing in terms of energy. I like to picture the river taking away any stress or confusion I feel and replenishing the earth around it as it goes.

But a river could *also* carry a spell away. Delivering faster than I could on my own.

This is all I need in an apartment. I do most of my research and admin tasks for the shop from my velvet mustard-yellow couch, and I've never needed more than one bedroom. It's a cozy place for a single person.

Tonight, I can't help but notice just *how* cozy it is. Another person couldn't live here. Well—they could, but we'd be on top of each other, and probably sick of each other within a week.

For the first time, it occurs to me that this apartment might not be enough for the rest of my life. How am I to envision Finley on my sofa, with the colorful patterned rug beneath the wooden coffee table made of a single slab of raw wood and iron stand beneath. *Surely he'll need a leather chaise across from my sofa.* The thought stops me in my tracks. *Oh, I can see him here.*

When I moved back, I thought I'd keep the apartment for six months and look for a house during that time, but nothing ever called to me. There wasn't any reason to get a bigger house when the shop's inventory could stay in the house and there was no one else to share the space with. I added my modern art prints covering most of the walls with splashes of color in antique frames. I think cozy eclectic would describe the small place. As I step back, I try to imagine a leather chaise and it simply wouldn't fit.

Perhaps it is time to move. When you have a desire, you must make room for it in your life. Show the universe that you are ready.

I take off my coat and hang up my bag, looking at my place with fresh eyes. It's neat and clean with tidy secondhand furniture, most of which I got from estate sales. I've made it into a home, but it's a home that's starting to look like it could be packed up any second.

I'm getting *way* ahead of myself. Time to take a step back and sit on a cushion I keep near my balcony window. It's too cold to crack the window but I can just barely hear the soothing breeze.

I replay everything that happened in the library, with an intent on simply observing.

For some reason, I keep imagining it from the far corner of the aisle, behind my table. That's where that sound came from, didn't it? I'd swear on my life I heard a gasp.

Maybe it wasn't a gasp. Maybe it was an echoed

whisper from another person in the library, traveling along the shelves until it got to me.

But I can't stop picturing me and Finley from that distance, as if I was also leaning over the table, holding my breath as I watched.

We were so close together.

If I'd stumbled or leaned, I'd have leaned right into him.

I picture Finley's face as he held his breath. That's when he must've started blushing, because his cheeks were pink when our hands touched. I swear they were. And the memory stirs a warmth within me.

And there's me, staring up at him in awe. In my memory, the energy between us was palpable. A force pulling us together. I can still feel it now. I close my eyes relishing it.

From this mysterious viewpoint, it seems that way, too. I'm leaning into it, starting to lift my heels from the floor, and Finley exhales and leans toward me, and then—

A shiver rushes across my shoulders. It's closer to a cold breath than a gust of wind, but my skin prickles all over my body, and I leap up from the cushion.

"There was something there," I say to my apartment. The white mushroom lamp on my side table turns on, startling me, but it's fine—I have it on a timer, so it'll be on when I get home. I'm only here early tonight because Finley touched me. And then he invited me to look at the library's collection of rare books and records.

That's *definitely* something.

I just *know* that tonight was important. It couldn't be clearer if somebody had written it in lipstick on my bathroom mirror. It's time to cast my own spell.

And as if I knew it would be needed, there's a candle sitting out on my countertop on a small black plate.

My heart ticks up. I'd been meaning to set intentions for the transition into winter, but for whatever reason, I didn't get around to it. I left my box of matches out, too. The box of matches is nearly empty and it's then that I smirk at the design on the two sides. One being the death tarot card and the other the lovers. How fitting.

Before snatching the candle, I reach under the sink cabinet and tear off a bit of paper from a brown bag.

"You'll do," I whisper.

Goosebumps brush down my shoulders as I stand straighter. My little apartment kitchen is alive with energy, like I'm standing in the center of a circle made up of coven members, all of them sending their energy into me.

It's completely possible that they met here hundreds of years ago, and their intentions were so powerful and focused that I can still feel the echoes of them, even now. Perhaps they are my guides. I know not every detail of what lies on the other side, but at this moment I feel as if it's meant to happen. The calm power is a bright white light that surrounds me.

I take the candle, matches, and paper back to my living room and bring my cushion over to my coffee table. The table is set up with a small stack of books, a chunk of clear quartz sitting proudly on top. And a little selenite bowl of small crystals. Quickly, I snag the rose quartz and slip it into my bra. Casting spells never looks as dramatic as it does in the movies, but my heart pounds anyway. The chill of the rock against my heated skin does nothing to calm the adrenaline racing through me.

I cross my legs on the cushion and close my eyes again. With my left hand over the crystal, my right still holds the candle, and I move it back and forth between my thumb and forefinger.

Casting spells is something I take seriously. The

only thing more serious is casting a spell meant to directly influence another person. I avoid that whenever possible, because you can never fully control the impact of a spell on others. You don't know their life's purpose or the details of what they've been through. The spell can twist and turn in ways you never imagined, and the wrong spell could come back on you in a form you didn't predict. I decided long ago that I would rather avoid spells for those who do not consent.

As I concentrate, though, the answer comes into my mind, clear as a bell.

*Cast on Finley. It is him you crave, and the energy running through this town is far more dangerous than influence.*

I ask myself whether this is true three times, leaving plenty of time for a feeling of dread or foreboding to come over me, and it never does. Perhaps I can word it in a way where it is to show me. Center myself.

Finally, I'm settled enough to reach for a pen on the shelf underneath the coffee table.

I write *the truth of love could not be more obvious* on the paper and roll it into a tiny scroll. If he desires me, I will know it without doubt. The highest of feelings he has for me are shown to me and only me. I do not wish to change his heart, only for me to know it.

That's the heart of this spell. It's not to force Finley to do something that's wrong for him, or that he doesn't want to do. It's not to change him in any way. It's to bring clarity to the tension between us and let us both see what's possible before we go any further. *Before I move from my apartment and buy a leather chaise.* At that thought I snag the dark blue sodalite from the small bowl in front of me.

"For clarity," I whisper and then gently place it beside the iron plate.

Then I light the candle and watch the flame burn into the dark for a few moments, breathing deep. I stare at the flame and whisper once more, "For the good of all and to the harm of none, let me clearly see the feelings he holds for me." The air around me is practically vibrating. I wouldn't be surprised if a spirit actually materialized—that's how real the energy feels.

I believe in this spell. I believe in what I feel. It's as real as the library or my apartment.

"For the good of all," I begin, my voice steadier than I feel. "And to the harm of none, do what you must to make Finley realize his feelings for me." I'm speaking to everything as I cast. All the forces in the universe that could bring us together or keep us apart. I'm speaking to energy and fate and destiny, and I can almost hear it listening. I can hear how it's holding its breath to catch every word.

"Let him feel the most intense and highest feelings of passion that are possible in this lifetime for us. Let him understand them and see them clearly. I —I want it now." A lump appears in my throat, and my voice falters. I didn't realize how much I wanted this until I spoke those words. I tried to tell myself I was only *interested* in Finley, but I was lying to myself. I'm more than interested. What's between us feels as old as fate, and I need to know if he feels that, too.

"I need to know," I admit to myself and to my spell. "Show us both if he is capable of wanting me and loving me. Make him feel this knowledge in the depths of his bones. Make me feel it in the depths of my soul. Make me know." The energy in my living room swells, and the hairs on the backs of my arms stand up. Whatever power is listening to my spell, it knows I'm almost finished. It knows there's only one more element to add—the element of *time*. It might be the most important element, because without clear boundaries, the spell could take longer than a lifetime to work. "Make me know by tomorrow's eve."

I hold the tiny scroll with *truth of love* written on it above the candle flame, and it catches immediately. The scroll turns to ash on the iron plate, and the energy in the room seems to tighten around me until it takes my breath away.

Then, just as suddenly, it releases.

I know there's no gust of wind in my apartment.

I know there aren't even any open windows.

But there *is* a puff of air, like someone whistling, and the candle goes out.

---

## 3

# FINLEY

The library is vacant.

I know it for a fact.

The teens who came in to work on a group project left to go get food at the diner. They couldn't have announced their decision louder. The weekly stitch-and-bitch club, a group of "feisty" grandmothers, left at six to go have a glass of wine at the bar. Nobody else has been in.

Yet, someone's watching me.

Their eyes burn on my back, giving me a sense of unease. *Someone is here.* It makes the hairs on my neck stand over and over again. That's not the kind of feeling anyone would be able to chalk up to paranoia or an overactive imagination, and certainly not me. Not after years of being here.

I've worked in the library long enough to know someone is watching, and that someone is dead. I swallow thickly, running my forefinger down the edge of the ancient text laid out on the counter.

The library is haunted. For as long as I can remember, the spirits reside in the depths of the shelves. It took a long time for me to be still when one is felt. A longer time to communicate, to understand, and to not be startled. This presence is notable though.

The library is housed in one of the oldest, most-active buildings in the entire town. A section of the floor down the aisle that's nowhere near where I'm standing creaks as if the building can hear me thinking about it. My eyes shift as goosebumps flow down my shoulders.

I stack the old books in the crook of my elbow and leave the circulation desk with easy strides. The reaction is instant. My breath shortens and a chill races down my spine, and the feeling of being watched—being closely followed—gets so strong that I almost react.

I don't turn around, though.

It's a game these ghosts play, I think. They used to startle me. They still try to do so. My lips kick up in an asymmetric smirk.

There are other games they could play if they wanted to drive me crazy or run me out of town, but other than a few books thrown off the shelves and doors opening and closing when they're not supposed to, nothing ominous has happened.

Other than the general haunting. They simply exist and want their presence known. Perhaps that gives them comfort.

Clearing my throat and pushing my shoulders back, I step into one of the aisles to reshelve borrowed books that have been returned. Movement flickers in the corner of my eye, but I pretend I didn't see it.

Some spirits or ghosts don't *want* to be looked at, and they'll use the shadows to their advantage. You'll see a creepy face when you don't want to, or a figure that doesn't look right, and then you'll never be able to unsee it.

I've worked here long enough to know better.

Long enough to know all about the history of the building, and how it was originally the town hall.

That's where the leaders of the town would go to meet and decide issues of the day. It sounds innocent enough when you phrase it like that, but there have been times when the leaders of the town—

mostly the older men—would decide to go after people who scared them.

They'd decide to go after women they could easily label witches. I've only seen one of the women once. But sure enough, I knew it was her because I'd spent that week reading about the trials. I knew her face when I saw it. She came and went, perhaps at peace with someone in this realm understanding the horror of what had happened. And knowing she was innocent.

She was the first, but not the last. Some come and go, others, like the one behind me, stay. What they crave from their hauntings, I do not know.

The heavy book in my left hand is a record of town meetings. In buildings like this one, sometimes there would be debates that turned into arguments. Some of those arguments even turned bloody. Passionate and emotional energy was expended here when this was the town hall, and that was before it was the courthouse.

I can't tell you how much justice was actually done in these walls, but justice wasn't the *only* thing done here. Corruption and lies and fear form a long-lasting layer over the original hardwood.

More of the boards creak as I cross to the opposite side of the main hall.

There are rows of bookshelves in the largest study room with my circulation desk in the center, more toward the front. The aisles are narrow so we can fit as much shelving as we need to house the library's collection, but none of the aisles are as narrow as the one in the very back.

It's probably against some building code to have an aisle that narrow, but nobody who's in charge of enforcing those codes ever does anything about it. It's where I feel the most presence. Where so many spirits hide. Tucked away with the history of this place.

Whenever the fire marshal comes around, he avoids the aisle in the back like someone tiptoed their fingers down his spine and blew between his vertebrae.

They probably did.

They've done it to me.

With my shoulders squared, I silently go from aisle to aisle and stack to stack. The sensation of eyes on the back of my neck gets stronger, then lets off, then gets stronger again. I remind myself to breathe deep and normal. My mind might be used to the fact that the library I spend most of my time in is haunted, but my body isn't.

I've been haunted by night terrors of death

before. Often waking and needing to know who it was and what exactly happened. The visions so real.

But other dreams have come, day and night, regardless of whether or not my eyes are shut. Dreams of comfort and gratefulness.

I am unsure of the spirit behind me. It's something that's old and wary, or maybe my age and devilish.

I don't know for sure. I don't know if I'll ever know for sure about these particular ghosts.

But I sure as hell *want* to know. The secrets of this town inspire the stories that come to me. Every moment I get, I write the thrilling short stories and give the spirits a way for their silent screams to be heard. I've written seven now under a ghost pen name. No one knows it's me and no one needs to know. It matters to me though. To hear their tales, tragic and otherwise, and share what they wish to be known.

A footstep scuffs on the floor behind my back. Out of instinct I almost forget and turn around, but I don't. I move along the back aisle instead, to the place where Hazel touched my hand earlier today. A warmth flows through me at the thought. A short groan threatens to leave me as my eyes close.

I cannot think about her without getting hard.

It's an instant reaction. I brace myself with a hand on the shelves, close my eyes, and inhale the scent of her.

It's been hours and hours since she was here, and the library is full of old books and older wood and stone. With the heat all the way on for the recent cold snap, all I should be able to smell is warm radiator.

But there she is. The scent of her teasing me.

My eyes open slowly as a thought hits me: Is it the ghosts playing a trick on me?

I can feel them getting closer. They don't have to be able to read my mind to see the effect Hazel has on me.

She's had that effect for a long time, ever since she first walked through the door of the library years ago. Her presence is calming and yet all-consuming. She's beautiful and intelligent and of all the people in this town, she would understand, I think.

How my life changed when my parents passed, how I hid in books as a child. How I searched for them and yet found myself here. They're gone, and I am at peace with that. What I'm left without them is a gift most do not have. Peace with the dead and an energy that welcomes spirits. They have comforted me, befriended me in some ways. And given me powers I cannot explain.

The living do not intrigue me as much. Or at least they didn't used to. But then she came in. *Hazel*.

It was like lightning struck me when I first saw her. The shock kept me still. She was there, between the two aisles that everyone else avoids. The aisles where the spirits rest. And she was at home there, searching through the texts for a story I might have already known.

And I...didn't make a move. I merely watched. What was she doing and why did they give her peace in their home here. I had to know, but I didn't even know her name.

It was easy enough to get her name from some of the ladies in the knitting club, and even easier to find out that she took over the Bewitched Boutique, and even easier to walk down the street on one of my breaks and glance in the window of her shop.

The bells chimed as I came in for a cup of coffee in the corner of her shop. It didn't take long for me to feel comfort with her as well. The allure is addictive. Watching her in the library on dark nights. Sharing stolen glances. I'm sure she understands the dead in the way I do.

Hazel has been studying the history of the town, and its most well-known coven, for as long as she's been here.

I let out a curse into the books as the floorboards creak again. They know my fantasies of Hazel. They know what she does to me.

I've thought of a thousand different ways to approach her, and none of them seemed right. She doesn't come here for me, and I don't wish to startle her and scare her away as the ghosts do to others.

But then today...

She came in, and I *felt* it. I felt curiosity coming off her in waves. I've felt it before, but I didn't want to assume it was about me no matter how many times I caught her looking.

Today, I knew. I can still feel her fingers brushing against mine like it's still happening. This darker side of me is only one aspect of my life. Of course I have a life to share with someone. Friends and a home where I host parties and poker nights. With a PhD in archival studies and the occasional course at the local universities, I have a life I could share with another. They'd never have to know this secret of mine. But I've never wanted someone only to hide from them. Then there's her and I just know if I were to tell her, she would understand. Although I fear I'll scare her. It is not often I think of her so much. I close my eyes and grip the edge of the counter, there's something in the air tonight.

"I have to do something for her," I say out loud, then pick my head up. "What, though?"

I slide one book into place, then another, and just as I'm about to shelve the last one, an old, black book no taller than my hand jostles out from the titles around it. My body stills.

This book is one of my favorites. It's a romance from another era. From the *coven* era. One of the women wrote it and had it hand-bound, and somehow it made its way from her house to her granddaughter's house to this library. A romance book; *romance her.*

"Thanks," I say to the ghosts, who don't give any hint that they heard me.

I slide the last book in its place on the shelves, then take the old, leather bound romance up to the circulation desk.

I pull the antique carved-wood chair out from under the desk and take a seat.

Then I take out my grimoire. My scribbled notes of the stories they've told stare back at me. As do the sketches.

My grimoire is a simple watercolor sketchbook. Nothing obnoxious or suspicious. Merely a home to my thoughts and notes, and summonings of sorts. The pages are thick enough that I can write with ink and add illustrations if I need to, but to everybody else, it's just a sketchbook—not worth stealing, not worth a glance.

I flip through a few pages, and the sketchbook falls open to exactly the spell I need for tonight. A chill flows through me as I read it over as if confirmation.

"She'd love this. Wouldn't she?" I say beneath my breath.

It's a spell that allows someone to feel what the writers felt while they were writing the book. It lasts as long as the candle is burning, and all you need to do is touch whatever book you want to experience. The spell awakens the spirit of the writer for as long as the flame still burns on the wick. She can experience the intensity of what the spirits wished to be known. Bringing them more to life for only a moment.

I could offer this gift to her. I could show her this side of me and see if she would enjoy this thinly veiled realm of life and death as I do.

If she desires more, I could give her so much

more. I could give her anything and everything she could possibly want. Tomorrow night, I'll see exactly what she thinks of me and exactly what she desires.

## 4

## HAZEL

I'm late. I'm *late*! How am I running late for the only date I've ever been truly excited about in all my life?

Everything was going fine all day, except that I couldn't sleep last night. My mind would not shut off and my body was vibrating with excitement. My own anticipation of the very clear deadline I'd given the spell kept me up all night.

It made me anxious a bit as well, because that was bold, wasn't it? Ordering the universe to show me the truth of his love in *one single day*? Bold but effective, I think.

What's done is done, but that didn't make it any easier to fall asleep.

Then, because I hadn't slept, I woke up late,

smacking the alarm like it had some audacity to pull me from my slumber. It seemed earlier than it was because thick clouds were covering the sky. It was the kind of morning that didn't seem to know if it wanted to rain or not, so I drove to the shop instead of walking.

And then I spent all day losing track of what I was doing. As if my mind was preoccupied, unable to focus on a thing. I shelved an entire shipment of crystal necklaces in the wrong part of the store *and* in the wrong order and had to redo them. A group of women on a tour of the area came in while I was halfway through the sandwich I got for lunch, and I rang two of them up backward and had to start over.

It was like the store *wanted* me to call it quits and close early.

But then what would I do? Show up to the library and hang around in my car, waiting for it to close? I may be a touch obsessed, called to Finley in a way I can't explain, but I don't want that to be obvious. And if I wasn't working I would be consumed with the idea of tonight. Throughout the day all I can think is how obvious it is that the spell worked. It's as if the intention has woven itself around my being. Tightening as the day has gone on. Perhaps a piece of the spell has bound itself to me. Or maybe it's a different spell, one from fate. I cannot know.

Since the library closes *after* the store, I made a point of staying open late.

And then, of course, a group from the paint-and-sip on the other side of the downtown area came in two minutes before I was ready to lock up, and I did my best not to rush them.

Half an hour. They spent half an hour browsing, which I knew was possible but really hoped wouldn't happen. Late for my first date with Finley. My eyes closed with irritation but, at the very least, I am not desperately waiting for the library to close.

As soon as I closed the door behind them and flipped the sign, the clouds opened up and started pouring down rain. I could not believe it. The darkness that covered the sky and how the clouds seemed to open up.

And then the small light over my shop door flickered and went out. Sparked right before my eyes and the building across the street went dark at the same time.

As I drive down the cobblestone road to the library, I'm pretty sure the whole town is without power, which means the street lights aren't working, either.

I ease into the intersection, checking all four ways a million times, and wave back at a guy who's waving me through. Everyone has become very polite since the power went out, but that's making the drive to the library slower than walking would have been. The temperature outside is suddenly *just* cold enough to make the street slick, so traffic is at a crawl, and I swear, *everyone* is out tonight.

My heart races, and worries attempt to slip into my mind, but I shut them down. Tonight is going to go exactly as it should. I just know it. And perhaps I'm meant to come in a bit cold and a bit wet and in need of comfort.

I arrive at the library parking lot twenty minutes late. My heart skips a beat at how dark it is with the power out. The lights by the door aren't on, and it appears pitch black inside.

*Is he still there?* I wonder as the windshield wipers swipe one last time. I turn off the ignition and swallow down my nerves.

*Did Finley give up on me?* My heart flickers before I catch sight of a car in the parking lot. It must be his.

Shaking my head, I can't believe I even thought that. I cast the spell. I know tonight is going to show me how he feels and I know deep down there's something there. The car door shuts with a thud as I hurry across the lot and almost slip in a patch of rainwater on the sidewalk. I barely stop myself from falling so I slow *way* down even though the rain's wetting my hair and on the back of my neck. God, it's *cold*. I should have brought an umbrella, but I didn't think of it.

Grimacing, I make my way as quickly as I can. I climb the steps to the library doors breathing a little harder than I'd like. As if I've been holding my breath and now my lungs are struggling to catch up.

The building is old, and with the power out, it's as if I've stepped back in time before the invention of electric lights. The thought pushes a huff of a laugh from my chest.

I can't see my reflection in the windows set into the front doors at all. It's too dark. But I pat my hair anyway, attempting to smooth down any strays, stand up tall, and pull on the door handle. I most certainly look as though I've been caught in the rain for a minute, but it'll be alright. It's the fact that I'm late that concerns me most.

The door seems heavier tonight. It opens with a loud *creak*, and part of me wants to run back to the warmth of my car and hide there for a few minutes first. Part of me is that nervous. Part of me is that excited.

"I'm sorry I'm late," I call and step inside. My voice nearly echoes. "I was just—oh, *wow*." My entire body freezes.

There are a dozen candles lit on the circulation desk. Different sizes and heights. From a small jar, to a tea light, to an elegant two-prong candelabra. So many candles that it makes a ring of light. Finley stands behind the desk, lit with a warm glow.

My heart seems to flicker, to trip like I nearly did a moment ago. In black suit pants with a simple button-up cotton dress shirt, you'd think Finley would come off a bit nerdy or professional. But his sleeves are rolled up revealing the corded muscle in his forearms. The air around him is powerful and undeniably so. Again my heart stutters. Forgetting it's purpose of keeping me alive in favor of something else....in favor of lust, perhaps.

The next time my heart beats, I swear the heat and blood flow travel lower.

His dark eyes meet mine this time and he offers me a charming yet relaxed smile. "You came."

His voice. Good God what has overcome me? The spell was for him, but it must've affected me too. Slowly I slip my purse off my shoulder and make my way toward him, toward the glowing light, my heels clicking on the marble floors.

"I should've called, but I… There were people at the shop." My voice seems too loud at first, so I lower it and then clear my throat. A blush rises to my cheeks and I wish it didn't. The heat throws me off. I continue, "And I didn't want to kick them out, and everybody has somewhere to be tonight. Then this" —I gesture to the power going out—"I'm so sorry I'm late."

With the lights out, the bookshelves are only slightly darker shadows. It's romantic somehow but eerie all the same. Lightning flashes against the large floor-to-ceiling windows at the far back of the room and for a moment there's light and then it's gone.

"I'm glad you made it," Finley says softly, and then he steps out from behind the desk to meet me. His gait is just as powerful as his broad shoulders. It's a quiet authority and simultaneously charming. He picks up one of the candles, a tall pillar candle that could burn for hours on a handled drip pan, and escorts me past the desk. "This way. I set up a little something."

"Is that an antique?" I ask, because the brass candle holder he has definitely looks like it came from a century ago or more.

"Original to the building," he says with a slight grin. With the glow of the candles fading, he reaches out, this time his hand warm and comforting on my elbow, to lead the way. "I have a surprise for you."

I arch a brow. "Is it the books that are only available by appointment?" I'm only half joking.

"Yes." He laughs, low and amused. The handsome sound forces a smile to my lips. "But I have something else to show you, too."

My heart beats faster but I ignore it. Swallowing down my nerves I venture a guess. "More books?"

He chuckles again, leading me down a set of stairs in the back hall I've been down only a few times before. "In a way." The iron spiral staircase is large enough to not be dangerous but small enough to separate us from walking side by side. He takes my hand, and I can't escape the warmth of his touch.

With every step, my heart beats harder.

It's a heady feeling, to follow him by candlelight to the ancient books room. I'm certain that's where we're headed.

We walk together through the library, our footsteps echoing. Finley lets go of my arm to open a door in the middle of the back wall. It's easy to ignore most of the time because it's already locked, but this time, when he pulls it open—

I actually gasp.

This room is *full* of candles.

It's obvious he's taken care to place them where they can't tip over or damage any of the valuable books, but they're *everywhere*. The old wooden desk in the back has several lit on it. Candles in various heights line the back walkway. There's one window on the right side and tea lights sit on the windowsill.

The candles aren't the only difference though. The room isn't crammed with study tables, like it was when I got a glance inside my first year back. The two tables are gone, and there's a blanket on the floor along with book stands to hold more candles, a low table, and a few cushions.

"You must love candles," I breathe.

"The power went out," Finley says with an amused smirk.

I cringe at my comment. "Right, right. And here I was, thinking you just wanted to set the atmosphere." A nervous laugh leaves me and I'm very aware that my heart is damaging my chest. My brain is screaming at me not to blow it.

Finley drops his hand to my lower back, and a little charge goes through me. From the way he exhales, he felt it, too. His hand on my body like that sends a shock through my entire system. I need more of it. Desire races through my veins.

"Maybe I was," he teases. "Would you have liked it if I turned out all the lights?"

"As opposed to fate deciding for us?"

He laughs again, and this time it's hotter and more knowing. "Do you think it was fate that caused the power outage?"

"Maybe it was," I tease back, rocking slightly on my heels. Even through my coat and my clothes, I can feel the heat of his palm. It's way too early in the evening to press myself closer to him, but damn, I want to. "Maybe everything that's ever happened was all to lead us to tonight, exactly how it is." I try to say it casually, almost jokingly even, although I mean it. Everything happens for a reason.

"Nothing but moonlight and candles." He comments as we walk closer to the blanket.

"Very pretty I think," I comment and steal a glance at his sharp jaw line peppered with stubble. Oh how I wish to run my fingers down his jaw and kiss him.

"Yeah," he says, blowing out a breath, and I'm quick to avert my gaze so he can't read my thoughts. I'd meant to be lighthearted, but Finley seems relieved that I mentioned this fact about the moon so casually. "How long have you been practicing?"

"Do you mean...how long have I been researching?"

"No." I see his smile out of the corner of my eye. "I meant practicing." He pauses, looking right at me and seeing through the fake pretending. "It's been about eleven years for me."

*Witchcraft.* He wants to know how long I've been practicing witchcraft, because he's been doing the same thing. My bottom lip drops in surprise just slightly. I can't believe I never sensed that about him. I can't *believe* I never thought to bring it up. There were a million chances to drop it into conversation. I've spent hours and hours here hovering around the same shelves, looking at the same kinds of historical documents, gathering facts about the same coven.

And Finley knew that. He's known about the books I checked out. He handed me one of those books just yesterday.

Of course he would know.

Out of everyone in town, he probably knows the most about what I might be able to find, and I was crushing too hard to ask him about it directly.

*Is this it?* I think to the universe or fate or whoever is guiding the spell I cast last night. *Is this the moment of clarity? Because it feels like it might be.*

"Since college, at least seriously," I answer,

because he's just waiting patiently, like we have all night. He's in charge of opening and closing the library—I guess we *do* have as long as we want. "So, seven years? Eight?"

"That's a good number."

A smaller shiver goes down my spine. "I hadn't thought about this being my seventh year."

I bite my lip to keep from saying something totally inappropriate about how I mostly feel hot, overwhelming attraction right now so thinking or doing any kind of math is hard. Finley's hand is still on my lower back as if he's forgotten that he's touching me or he wants to touch me so badly that he can't bring himself to stop.

"This is beautiful tonight," I say finally, the words sounding high and breathless. "I love the indoor picnic by candlelight."

"The picnic comes later."

"Oh? So we're...using the blanket first?" The words slip past my lips before I can stop them.

His eyes flicker with amusement once again and then he says, "The surprise will be better if we're sitting down."

Oh, God. Are we going to make out on the blanket? Did he bring a blanket and cushions and candles into this little back room so we could make out? That would be...amazing.

If the intention I put out into the world has opened his mind to the possibility that I might be into him as much as he's into me. Light goosebumps start at my wrists and go up to my shoulders.

I can feel it again—that tension between us. If it had a sound, it would buzz like the lights in the library usually do. There's no buzz to distract us right now, though, and the small room is so quiet that I can almost hear my own heart beating.

"After you." Finley holds out the hand that's not on my back, and I nod to him, smiling reflexively, my face hot. It's an easy path to the blanket, and when I lower myself down, I discover there is more than one blanket, all folded to make it more comfortable.

He sits down across from me, and I can't help remembering how close we were in the aisle before. He's closer now, his knees almost touching mine. The scent of his cologne fills my lungs.

My fingers itch to touch him again so badly. I ring them around each other instead.

That, I think, would be the real proof. Touching skin to skin and not over clothes. That would tell me what I desperately need to know about this mysterious, quiet man who knows about witches and covens and history and might even have cast his own spell.

That makes my breath stutter for a second or two.

Our intentions have to be aligned, don't they? Otherwise my tires would've gone flat or someone would've rear-ended me on the way here or the power outage would have been a disaster and not a bump in the road.

And Finley wouldn't have waited so long. He'd have come to the conclusion I ghosted him and gone home for the night.

But he didn't, and nothing stopped me, and now I'm here. Now *we're* here.

Finley looks me in the eye. And one last time my heart flickers from the intensity of his gaze. "Ready?"

## 5

## FINLEY

I've never felt more obsessed with Hazel than when I go to a shelf that's mostly hidden in shadow to get a stack of books I chose. Her presence is heady. All-consuming even. I'm not sure if it was the wait, the doubt that she wasn't coming, or merely the anticipation of what's to come. The excited desire overrides even my need to breathe.

And the stolen glances she gives me. With a beautiful blush on her cheeks after being caught in the cold rain. My god. She is gorgeous and tempting in every way. It's making me crave more from her. I want to touch her skin, not just her clothes, and it's unbearable.

Silently, I scold myself. Pull it together.

When I turn around again, the flames on the

candles waver slightly, almost like a breeze came through the room. A breeze wouldn't *shake* the flames like that. I move with nervous anticipation. It feels as if everything is waiting for her pleasure.

This room has never felt quite like this before. Not even when the spirits were at their most restless. I call upon the magic here to impress her. I need to impress her tonight. *For her to fall for me as I've fallen for her.*

Clearing my throat, I shake my head to rid the thought. No woman has ever made me feel this way. This delicate balance of showing her all of me that I've not shown others while also needing her to accept it. I've never cared for the approval of others, but tonight feels different.

Hazel's gorgeous face glows in the candlelight. She has her knees drawn up to her chest, and she's watching me with beautiful doe eyes. It feels like a long walk back to the blanket, though it's only a few steps.

"Those are not books *in a way*," she says as I lower myself back down to the blanket. "Those are books literally."

"These are not *just* books," I scold teasingly. "These books are *history*."

"Are you going to read to me, then?" She smiles

and dimples show up in her cheeks. So fucking beautiful.

"I hadn't planned on it."

She crosses her legs instead, sitting up straighter. "What are we going to do with them?"

I answer in a single word, "Magic."

Hazel doesn't laugh as her eyes follow me. Perhaps she's testing me. Wondering how serious I am. Truthfully I don't know for certain how serious Hazel is with her craft. And how much she believes. But judging by her research and book selection. She'll understand and enjoy all that I have planned.

If the tension in the air is accurate, she's curious.

I gather my grimoire from one of the book stands, along with the single unlit candle in the room. I crave her touch so much it's hard to keep my hands off her. It's hard to put the books down and keep my focus on the spell.

Hazel folds her hands in her lap. Her gaze is even more palpable on my skin than the light touches from the spirits.

I wasn't planning to cast the spell in front of her, but it won't mean anything unless I do. Anyone else could've cast it, or it could be old magic that goes along with the building, and there's nothing stronger in me than the need to kiss her. To show her who I am.

I don't know why it's happening tonight of all nights when I've held myself back for so long, but I couldn't care less. I *have* to go with it. Nothing else would seem right. I'd be a coward if I didn't. I'm lucky enough to know that turning away from this—hiding anything from her—would be creating unfinished business.

I can't have that with Hazel.

As she watches, I light the last candle and begin the spell.

This one isn't open-ended. It's not asking the universe to do something for me, like shield me from harm or keep someone else from coming close.

This spell is about calling the spirits to return. Those who wish to be known. Those who are drawn to Hazel as I am. To impress her and please her. I can give her this gift when no one else can.

Books are the finest tools to call spirits back because the stories inside are made of the author's being. Everything that made them who they were. Their souls sewn into the text of the pages. The candle flame acts as a timer. So long as it is lit, the spirit is welcome.

I finish the spell.

Hazel doesn't say anything. Although her eyes hold so many questions.

She keeps her gaze on my hands as I set the candle aside.

"Now what?" she whispers.

"Touch one of them." I dare her and my heart races. I've done this before. I was enraptured by the stories of ghosts from long ago. I could taste the tincture they took to heal. I could smell the burning of the fire they lit in the coldest nights. I could feel their presence.

"If you want to meet them," I add.

Hazel reaches forward, hesitating for a second, then choosing the top book on the stack. I was careful about the books I chose. Only books I've read, spirits I've felt comfortable with in the past years.

She brings it close to her body, biting her lip.

I can feel the intention of the spell circling us and the books. The spirits aren't always visible, but I hope they will be. *Impress her*. I plead with them.

Just this once, allow her to know what I do.

The hair on my nape stands up, and I brace for the magic to surround Hazel.

Nothing happens.

She lets out a breath. "Is there anything else I

should do," she asks, a note of disappointment in her voice.

"Try the next one." I offer and make myself comfortable on the blanket around her. It takes time. Afterall, it's only an offering. The ghosts must accept.

Hazel lays the first book carefully aside as if she wants to remind it that it's still important, even if the spell didn't work immediately. Her thumb caresses the worn leather and as she lifts the second volume from the pile, her right hand remains on the first. As if not wanting to let go.

I recognize the handmade paper of the one she now holds. This one was written by a soldier who fought in World War I. It's a diary that reads like a novel. He had a way with words, which isn't a surprise. A man who never found love and was far too wounded to think himself worthy of it until his dying days.

"His maternal grandmother was part of the coven you've been studying." I speak the fact beneath my breath. As if afraid to give too much away.

Hazel's brow arches. "You've been keeping track of what I'm studying?" Her tone is teasing. I love it.

"You visit the same shelves every time. You're the only one who's brave enough to sit at that table."

"It's just a table," she says with a little laugh. I love the way her shoulders shake slightly when she laughs. "Why would it take bravery?"

"The ghosts make some people nervous."

She watches me for a beat, probably to see if I'm joking. Is that a blush on her cheeks? Her lips part just slightly as if she's wanting to say something, but she doesn't. The flickering candlelight makes it hard to see, but that blush is as evident as it is beautiful.

My face is hot, too. I've never spoken to anyone about the spirits here. Over the years I've learned some souls simply don't believe in ghosts. So I keep it to myself. But this is something I could share with her. I'm sure of it.

I don't know what's happening to me. Suddenly it seems important for her to know the depths of my knowledge, too. I know she reads about a long-ago coven. She spends hours nearly every night craving their tales and to know what's real. I've felt the spirits here and I know they're not some trick of my mind. I know it's all real—the magic and the spells and the ghosts.

"This place is haunted." Hazel states although her tone makes it sound like a question. She's confirming it for herself. She must have sensed it, and why wouldn't she have? She's been looking into the supernatural truth of this town for years. I merely nod and she answers, "I knew it."

My lips kick up into a smirk.

Hazel holds the book closer to her chest, her eyes fluttering closed.

I want to kiss her so much. I've never felt such a pull to another.

"Maybe you're not in the mood," Hazel says to the book, her voice soft. She lays it aside. "Next one?"

I almost forgot about the spell altogether. "Go ahead."

She never gives up hope. Touching one book after the other. Holding them, reading the first page or flipping through the pages.

By the time she gets to the last one, my head is spinning with disappointment.

I needed this to *work*. I needed to *show her what I did*. I needed to *impress her*, so she knows I—

My thoughts cut out.

Hazel gently places the last book on top of the stack she made, and I can see her prepare to tell me "it's fine."

It's not fine, but I'd almost believe it, coming from her.

"Have you eaten?" I ask, before she can say a word.

"I haven't," she says, running her fingers through her hair.

"Then it's time for a picnic." Quickly, I grab two bags that I stowed to the side. They're not as aesthetically pleasing as a wicker basket would be, but wicker baskets don't keep cold food cold and hot food hot. These thermal bags do.

Hazel scoots closer as I set out the plastic containers. They're mostly finger foods that go with wine—cheese, apple slices, crackers, and sliced meats—but also imported chocolates and specialty spreads. A bit upscale. I also pull out melted chocolate for dipping.

"Oh my god," Hazel breathes. "How did you get it to stay melted?"

"A spell that actually works," I tell her with a wink. There *is* a spell on the container, but I don't expect her to believe me when the spell on the books completely failed. "And," I say, pulling out the mug warmer I keep on my desk, "a mug warmer as backup."

Her eyes light up with her smile. "I *love* those things. I keep one behind the counter at the shop. It's the only thing that keeps me going when—"

"When it's below zero," I finish with her.

Hazel laughs. "You get me."

"I do." I move closer on the blanket so our knees are touching. "There are things I'd enjoy getting to know about you though."

"Is that right?" she asks beneath her breath. It's impossible to miss the desire in her eyes.

I set the mug warmer and chocolate at my side and open a container of strawberries. Then I hold one up in front of her so she can see it.

Hazel watches, her eyes sparkling.

I dip the strawberry into the chocolate, then take her chin in my left hand. Her skin is warm and when she parts her lips, my cock hardens.

She closes her eyes. For a second, I don't know if I can take it. I'm desperate for her.

But instead of laying her down on the blankets, I bring the strawberry to her lips and watch her teeth sink into the berry.

Hazel bites daintily through the flesh, leaving only a thin sliver of red and the leaves behind. Her tongue darts out to catch the juice, and fuck me, I want nothing more than to kiss her. To taste her and have my own dessert.

"Oh," she says, covering her mouth with her hand. "That's delicious. Where did you get it?"

"A place downtown."

On the second strawberry, when I take her chin in my hand, she puts her hand on my wrist.

Hazel waits, her eyes closed and her mouth open, for me to feed her the strawberry.

There's a tiny drop of chocolate at the corner of her mouth.

"You have something..." I gesture vaguely at my own mouth, but she just closes her eyes and lifts her chin toward me.

I can't resist it. I just can't. She obviously wants me to touch her, and I want to touch her so bad I might die from it before we leave this room, so I rest my fingers on her cheek and swipe the pad of my thumb over her full bottom lip, slowly, all the way to that droplet of chocolate.

Then I press my thumb to her lips.

Hazel takes my thumb into her mouth and sucks lightly at the chocolate.

I make a sound I'm not expecting in the back of my throat.

Hazel doesn't let go quickly. She lets my thumb slip between her lips, and then we're just staring at each other. I can't look away.

That's when all the candles flicker and then go out.

## 6

## HAZEL

When the candles go out, the back room at the library is pitch dark. Fear wraps itself around me at first. The darkness is unsettling. But Finley's here. Holding me, and for some reason, I'm wrapped in more curiosity and excitement.

Usually, the lights would be on in the main room, so we'd have some leaking in around the old door in its frame.

Now, without any power in town, much less the library, it's like trying to see through ink. The only reason I know Finley is still in the room is that I can hear him breathing, and his hands are on me, both gripping my shoulder and my hand.

"Finley..." I whisper, waiting for my eyes to adjust to the dark.

I'm warm, maybe even hot. My heart flutters and a nervousness comes over me. I'm so turned on I can hardly catch my breath. Something's happened.

My heart skips a beat.

"Hazel," Finley says. His voice is low and holds something to it. Something on edge and yet in a way that's desirable.

And then there are voices. So odd. So shockingly close I grip onto Finley's hand a bit harder.

The voices aren't very clear. Am I really hearing someone hold a conversation outside the library somehow? That would be possible in my apartment, where the walls aren't very thick, but the library's walls are made of thick stone from its earlier lives as the town hall and the courthouse. We shouldn't be able to hear chatter from a floor up and outside.

Confusion slips in but only for a moment.

They're too muffled, cutting in and out like bad cell service, and there's something about them...

A light comes on.

It's been so dark that I put my hand up to shield my eyes, but as I blink, letting them adjust, reality sinks in: it's not the candles.

Finley hasn't lit the candles, and the power hasn't

come back on. It's the spell. Not mine. It's Finley's. Holy fuck. Shock freezes my entire body.

This is a glow like I've never seen before, and it's coming from three ghostly spirits. Apparitions that form right before our eyes. "Finley," I whisper to him as he pulls me in close.

"It's alright, my little witch," he whispers in such a way that it soothes any terror that joined the shock.

I did *not* think of ghosts like this. I thought of figures under sheets at Halloween or old people walking the same hall night after night.

I did not think of...hot men. Their abs etched. Their shoulders are broad and their eyes... beautiful. Their eyes are the most detailed and striking. Almost ethereal.

I swallow thickly, wondering if I'm having visions.

"You see them?" Finley asks.

"Yes," I can only answer in a single word. My breath seems to fail me.

Their clothes don't make sense. One minute, they look like they're in uniform. The next, trousers and shirts. Either the ghosts can't decide how they want to dress from moment to moment or that's my own mind trying to make them into a form I can understand.

One of the ghosts has short, light hair. The middle ghost has longer dark hair pulled back from his face. The third has hair that might have been red falling into his eyes.

They're all looking at me.

"Hello," I say, because nobody's said anything and it seems like the right thing to do. "Who are you?"

The sound of the voices comes back. But they aren't clear enough.

"I'm sorry, I—I couldn't hear."

The middle one—with the longer dark hair—tips his head back and laughs. It's a rich, deep sound and sexy. My God, his tone and the smirk he wears. I hold Finley closer, wondering what he makes of all this. Is this what he intended?

Then the ghost gestures at the other two on either side of him, and they come closer. Close enough that I press against Finley, unsure, and he soothes me. Petting my hair and telling me it's alright before kissing my temple.

The oddest thing is that I believe him. Truly and deeply.

The redheaded ghost's foot brushes against the container of chocolate, and it rocks on the mug warmer.

Finley leaves my side only to grab the stack of books in one arm and the candle, which has somehow lit once again, in his other hand, then reaches to put them out of the way and off the blanket. He leans back in for the mug warmer and the remains of the picnic. One of the ghosts glances down at him, then closes his eyes.

The tables and book stands slide back from the blanket, leaving enough room for all of us. There's no noise as they move, apart from the creaking of the old desk. Chills flow down my spine and then lower. Somehow the fear of the ghost's power is directly linked to my clit. Perhaps it's the shock. Or the way Finley seems to greet the ghosts like old friends.

Finley gets to his feet at the same moment the dark-haired ghosts offers me his hand.

"You're a ghost," I tell him and feel foolish.

He simply smiles at me, leaning his head to the side as if to mock me. My stomach swoops. I *believe* in ghosts. I believe in energy and power and intention. If he wants to be able to help me up, he'll be able to do it, right?

And if *I* want him to be able to help me up...

I put my hand in the ghost's hand.

To my surprise, it feels as solid as Finley's hand, but much, much cooler and the icy touch has me pulling back before fully grasping his hand. The chills come back and wrap around me. My nipples pebble, and judging by the looks on the ghosts' faces, they can tell I'm… aroused. My cheeks go ablaze with a blush as I glance at Finley. He has nothing but approval and desire written in his expression.

I reach out once again, the ghost ever patient, and take his hand. The ghost doesn't give me an icy shock. It's more like stepping into an unheated pool. A stronger shiver goes through me, but I could get used to it.

The ghost is even hotter now that we're only a few inches away. Despite the chill of his hand, I'm heating up, too. I press my thighs together just for the sensation. "Finley," I practically moan and then watch him grip his cock from outside of his pants. "Fucking hell, Hazel," he groans under his breath. "I don't want to share you but for tonight I'll make an exception."

My bottom lip drops as I stare back at Finley.

"They can hear your thoughts, and I can hear what they're thinking," he says as a way of an explanation. "Don't be embarrassed. If this is what you want, I'm willing to give it to you tonight," Finley says and with wide eyes I stare back at him.

*Thump, thump, thump*, my heart races.

Finley chuckles deep and low at my hesitation before kissing me once on the lips. It's short and sweet and everything I've ever wanted. "Do what you want. Tonight is a gift for you."

I give in to that feeling and close my eyes before looking back at the ghosts.

"I want—" I start, my mouth dry.

The ghost kisses me. Getting closer.

He puts one hand on my waist and the other in my hair, tugs me to his body, and kisses me.

The dark-haired ghost is a confident kisser, and even while I'm kind of freaking out—because a ghost is kissing me, and he's good at it, and this has to be a dream—I'm also falling into it. Falling into this moment that can't be real.

That's the thought I hold onto. That and the offer from Finley. It's not real and I can do what I want. I reach for Finley as the ghost kisses me deeper, exploring me with his tongue. Even in my dreams, I crave him. I need him with me. I need to know he's alright with this. I lean my head back to break the kiss and peek at Finley to find him in awe, his eyes dark with lust. The ghost's lips drop to my neck and as a moan slips between my lips, Finley kisses me.

"You're so fucking sexy," he groans against my lips and his warmth at odds with the chill the ghost left behind is electrifying. I've never been so horny in my life.

Finley leaves my side and I'm barely able to watch him grab a lighter to light another candle and catch sight of the other two ghosts enjoying the show before the ghost is on me again. Kissing me.

It's the same cool feeling as his hands, and it only makes me more aware of how warm I am, and how much I've been craving being kissed like this, and touched…

And more.

As if he can hear my thoughts—because he can according to Finley—the dark-haired ghost lowers us down to the blanket. His grip is strong yet gentle, and as he lays above me, it's far more obvious how much taller he is. I grip his arm and feel nothing but hard muscle. In a blink his shirt is gone, nothing but the carving of muscle beneath my fingertips.

My God, he is gorgeous. As if I've imagined him myself.

The other two ghosts come with us. Finley steps in and nudges the dark-haired ghost out of his way, and then it's *his* hands in my hair and *his* mouth on mine. Possessively. And I fucking love it. The way he commands my body. His tongue massages mine and he steals my breath with his demanding kiss.

I let out a moan at the heat of him. He tastes a little like the chocolate he fed me and lets out a harsh breath when I arch up into him.

"Did you want me still?" I whisper, a hint of doubt creeping in although I tell myself again, it is only a dream.

"More than ever," he whispers back, and then both of us are stripping each other's clothes off as fast as we can. His hands are on my body and all the while, the ghosts watch.

The ghosts surround us, cool hands reaching past Finley to touch me. One grips my breast and then toys with my nipple. Another runs his fingers through my hair and the last kisses on the nape of my neck. The sensations are all-consuming. So much at once and yet far too little.

I need more. As Finley leans me back to kiss me, the two ghosts that haven't kissed me play with my nipples. Their groans of want fill my senses.

"Oh my god," I say into Finley's mouth. "Oh my *god*."

"You like that?" he asks. "You want more of that?"

"Yes," I manage to say in a single breath. "Please," I plea on the verge of coming already. "I've never—" I start to say and Finley tells me, "I haven't either."

Finley groans, pushing his hips into mine, then shifts himself off me so he's lying at my side. He slides his large, warm hand over one of my breasts and toys with my nipple, then lets the ghost have a turn.

For a moment I wonder what they're thinking. I wonder if they know exactly what I'm thinking. Flashes of them sharing me, one taking me from behind while I suck another, are so vivid in my mind.

I stare up at Finley and a sly grin grows on his face, "Oh Hazel..." he starts. "Such a naughty girl." Before the blush can spread any deeper in my cheeks, Finley nods to his right, to the ghosts waiting.

The dark-haired ghost pushes my thighs apart, then kisses down my belly. I open my thighs a little wider when he kisses my belly button and I turn my face toward Finley.

He leans down to me again, and then—

All I can feel is the wild sensation of being touched and played with by three ghosts and kissed by a man.

At the same time, the dark-haired ghost lowers his mouth to my pussy and licks. Oh fuck! The pleasure ignites through me. The cold and the heat at war along my skin. My heart is pounding, and my lungs are barely working.

I never thought I'd moan this loud in my life. On the sensitive, wet skin between my legs, the dark-haired ghost's tongue feels both hot *and* cold. I can't tell whether it's because I'm so wet and turned on or because the ghost is somehow drawing in heat to make it feel better for me.

It feels unbelievable. Almost as if I'll wake up in the morning and this will never have happened. But then Finley pinches one of my nipples, rolling it between his fingers, and I cry out, overwhelmed and loving it.

Cool fingers replace Finley's fingers again, and there's no *way* this isn't real. I can feel every touch down to my bones. I'm going to be able to feel this pleasure for the rest of my life.

"Please," I moan again, on edge of finding my release.

The dark-haired ghost licks up my slit and sucks on my clit, adding pressure until cool, ghostlike pleasure is shooting through all my nerves, all my veins, every part of my body.

"Yes, yes, yes!" I cry out and just then, Finley sends me over the edge by sucking my nipple into his mouth.

But the fall of the high doesn't come because they don't stop. My head wants to thrash, but I can't with Finley kissing me yet again.

For a beat, I'm frozen in the intensity. There are so many hands on my body. One of the other ghosts sucks at my other nipple. My hips rock, completely out of my control, as the third ghost breathes onto my neck, then kisses me there too.

My mind goes wild as the pleasure builds and builds and finally crashes over me once again. Back-to-back. This second one an even higher high.

I come hard at the same time I realize that Finley is finger-fucking me with two of his thick fingers as the dark-haired ghost licks me like he can actually taste me.

From the sound I hear him make, I think he might be able to. He gives me a deep groan of satisfaction, and I've never felt more powerful.

I'm already quivering from another swell of pleasure and none of them show any signs of stopping. The red-haired ghost pulls away from my nipple and jostles the dark-haired ghost until he agrees to switch places, and then the red-haired ghost is kissing up my inner thigh to the crease at my leg.

I spread my legs wider, not knowing what I want, only knowing that I want more. I get a glimpse of his smile, then he throws both my legs over his shoulders and goes down on me.

Finley finds my gaze, his eyes dark and his lips puffy from kissing me so hard.

"I wish you could see yourself," he says. "Fucking gorgeous."

"I need you," I'm able to moan, gripping onto him as my eyes flutter back with pleasure.

"Let us take our time," he answers, and instantly I'm overwhelmed with both a heady pleasure and the need for more.

Cold hands and warm ones travel all over my body and hold my legs open for the ghost and lift my ass so he can have access to more of me.

Finley puts his hand under my chin, and I open my eyes to see him watching me with fire in his eyes.

"Do you want them to fuck you?"

"Yes," I gasp. "God, yes. But I want you. I want *you.*"

That's the most important part of all of this. As much as I'm loving the attention of the ghosts, it only matters because it's happening with Finley. The desire I feel for them is the desire I have for him, only more, because I want more than anything to share this experience. I want us to have something that nobody else will ever have, and to be able to witness each other in it.

I'm getting everything I wanted. Everything I didn't even know I could want.

I part my lips to tell him that, but another orgasm steals the words out of my mouth.

He kisses me while I ride it out.

Finley's mouth is hot and possessive on mine, kissing me so intensely that it takes my breath away. All I can think is, *please*.

## 7

# FINLEY

The jealousy I feel as I watch Hazel come on the mouths and hands of three of the ghosts who have been haunting the library is like nothing I've ever felt before.

My body tenses with the need to fuck her. To claim her. To have her come on my cock.

I *know* these spirits. I don't know their faces or their names, but I know what their presence feels like in the library, and I know these are at least some of the spirits who have been trying to bait me into their games ever since I got here.

How could they resist her? It's what she wanted. But it's almost like watching a friend you trusted go after the girl you had a thing for when he *knew* you were into her.

Except this time, it's a ghost.

*Three* ghosts.

And they only want to impress her, as I requested. I did this. At war with my thoughts, I am delighted by her pleasure yet in need of having her first.

They do as I ask. They have permission for every touch.

If another man came into the library, interrupted our date, and kissed her in front of me...

The rage would be all-consuming. But I can't see her kissing another mortal. A mere man. This is different.

I invited them. I requested they impress her. I too wish for her wildest dreams to come true in this moment. Just this once. And then she's all mine.

Watching them play with her makes me harder for her. Perhaps I have a kink I wasn't aware of. Something that could make me feel even more for her than I already did.

I want to mark every spot on her that the ghosts touch. My mark. As the dark-haired ghost pulls back at her breast giving a *pop* as he releases her nipple, I clamp my lips down around it and flick it with my tongue until Hazel's gasping.

The two other ghosts switch places between her legs.

Which is where I long to be. Fucking her into these blankets until she's screaming my name. I've never needed anything more.

A pattering noise in the distance distracts me slightly. It takes me a minute or two, with Hazel arching up and moaning as the light-haired ghost drags another orgasm out of her, and the other ghosts finding every place on her body that makes her shiver.

It's raining harder. Thunder booms overhead. It's loud as fuck to make it through the roof and the building. A crackle of energy speeds through me like lightning. We can't see the flash from in here, but Hazel's hips jerk upward into me.

She can feel the same things I do.

I don't have to explain it to her.

I don't have to convince her that such a part of my life is real.

It should make me relieved, but instead it makes me want to claim her. In front of these ghosts and in front of *everyone*. I want my teeth marks on her neck. I need her to want me just as much as I want her. I need to please her. To hear her screaming my name as she comes undone.

As I position myself, Hazel has her head thrown back onto the blanket. Her thighs squeeze my sides as she takes a short breath, and then her voice gets higher as she comes.

I drag my cock over her slit, staring at her, and push two ghost-hands out of my way so I can grab her by the hips.

Hazel is so damn beautiful in the light from the ghosts. It makes her look ethereal, almost like she's a gift, and my heart skips another beat.

She lifts her hips again, another orgasm shaking her body. Even more than I need to fuck her, I need her to have what she wants. Whatever she wants.

I drink in the sight of Hazel breathing hard on the blanket, her thighs open for me, one arm thrown over her head and her other fisted in the blankets beneath us. She's so exposed like this. I can see almost all of her. Hazel hasn't hidden any of her pleasure, either, and that makes me want her even more than for her gorgeous body.

She's so obviously loving this. Relishing pleasure. Intoxicated by desire.

My mind is flooded with possibilities. With both of us working together, we could discover more of what the library's hiding. We could find other ghosts and other histories. I see her by my side. I fucking love it. I need it. I need her now.

I give myself another few seconds to memorize the scene.

One of the ghosts bends his head to her neck, kissing her there, then puts his hand around the front of her throat.

"Oh," my witchy girl breathes, and that's it. That's all I can take.

I line myself up and thrust into her with reckless abandon, bracing myself over her as I do. One swift stroke and she's mine. Her bottom lip dropped with a silent scream of pleasure.

Hazel's quick to put her arms around my neck as I fuck into her again. She's so fucking wet. So fucking hot. *There's no foreplay like ghost foreplay*, I guess, and I'm the only one who gets to feel the full effect of it. The thought fuels me to fuck her harder and deeper. She's hot and tight around me, made for me, and I get up on my knees and fuck her like I've wanted to since the second I saw her.

Hazel doesn't need me to slow down.

"Yes," she moans. "Finley, *please*."

The thunder gets louder, like it's in the building with us. The bangs and flashes of light accompany the sight of the ghosts playing with her. Touching and kissing, nipping and sucking. All over her body as I push her higher and higher. Closer to her release.

One of the ghosts slips his hand between me and Hazel and circles her clit while I fuck her. She clenches around my cock and I fucking love it. "Come on my cock," I command her. "Be my good girl and come."

The sound she makes is a muffled cry of pleasure, and I can barely hear it because the rain and thunder are so loud. She comes again and then again on my cock.

"Do that again," I order her. "Do that again, my little witch. One more time."

I lower my mouth and rake my teeth down her neck. Sucking and nipping, joining in the fun of toying with her as she gets off.

She cries out my name as she pulses around me, coming as hard as she did the first time.

"I love you," I tell her, fucking her through it, finding my own release. The pleasure rocks through me. "I want nothing more than you to come on my cock every night."

"*Yes*," she cries breathlessly and just then there's a blinding light.

The room gets as bright as a lightning flash, but

it's not lightning. It's the ghosts. She writhes underneath them, and I keep myself inside her to the hilt. The cold whips over me and between us.

*Is it time?* I find the dark-haired ghost on his knees next to me.

He leans down between me and Hazel and gives her one last kiss on the lips. It's quick and soft.

Then he sits back, locks eyes with me, and I nod in gratitude.

The ghosts disappear.

We're back in the dark once again, and I can't see a damn thing. Her heavy breathing and soft touch are everything to me in this moment. She clings to me, sated and trembling from the heated night of passion.

I rest my forehead on Hazel's. It takes a moment for me to catch my breath. For what just happened to truly register. Her hands find my shoulders, and we lie there for a moment, not saying anything. *Did I confess my love to her?* The thought hits me and I have to shove it down before I can overthink it.

A breeze slips through the room and as I grab the blanket to cover Hazel's bare skin, there's a sound like somebody blowing out a candle, except all the candles come to life again.

Suddenly there is light.

Hazel blinks up at me. Her hair's a messy halo, and she has my teeth marks on her neck, and she's perfect. Freshly fucked and beautiful. Needy still with those doe eyes.

"That was..." She starts but doesn't finish.

"Everything you wanted?" I question as I take her chin in my hand, forcing those beautiful eyes to look at me.

She only nods, staring up at me for approval.

"I'm glad but don't expect that with anyone else, understood?" I tell her and love how the command lights a spark in her eyes. She nods again.

My heart beats heavy and loud as I look down at her.

Just as I'm starting to tell her I meant what I said, there's a hum in the rest of the building. Light appears from around the door.

"The power's back on," Hazel says. "That means it's probably on everywhere else, too."

"That means we can go home."

"Your place or mine?" she asks.

"Mine."

## 8

## HAZEL

Finley lives close to the library, which surprises me.

Or maybe everything this evening has surprised me, and when we leave the library, I assume the rest of the night will be just as shocking. I'm ready to find out that he lives several towns away or in the middle of nowhere, but he helps me to his car, drives two blocks, and helps me back out again.

Back to reality. I can still feel their hands on me though. The pleasure still rocks through me. My mind whirls with what happened. Replaying each moment and with every thought, I look back to Finley. For approval and for the knowledge that he enjoyed it. For the knowledge that he still wants me. That come tomorrow morning, I'll still be his.

I don't know if I imagined it or not, but I think he said he loved me. In the heat of the moment, with an orgasm wrecking my body and mind, I could swear he said it.

With every moment, he shows his feelings. Opening the car door, holding my hand as he unlocks the door. And then wrapping his arm around my waist and kissing my temple when he flicks on the light.

His place has exposed brick. Shelves line the back wall and just as I imagined, a worn leather, nearly antique sofa sits on the far end of the living room.

My heart flutters. Like all of this is meant to be.

I'm so tired that I don't think I'll be able to stay awake, but then Finley strips naked to get into the shower, and I get a second wind.

He's gorgeous and has muscles etched like a Greek god.

"Come," he says, reaching his hand out and I obey. I love how he commands me. I love all of this.

My entire body is hypersensitive in the shower. I let Finley clean both of us up.

His thumb graces a few marks left from the night. Where I was nipped and sucked.

"Did you know they would—"

"No. I only asked them to impress you."

I clear my throat, that damn heat in my cheeks coming back even as the hot water sprays around us.

"I've never seen them like that before."

"How long have you known the library was haunted?" I ask. Partially to change the subject.

"From the day I had my interview."

Jealousy is written in his gaze and a possessiveness I've not seen before. I fucking love it. I have a feeling this night won't repeat itself and I'm just fine with that. I want Finley after all. And now I have him.

He smooths both hands over my hair, feeling to see if there's any conditioner that needs to be worked out. This man took the time to condition my hair, even though I know he's as exhausted as I am.

"You can...you can feel ghosts like that? Spirits? All the time?"

"Not all the time." He must not find any conditioner, because he runs his fingers through my hair one more time, then squeezes out the excess water. "There's something special about that building."

Silently, I agree. At least for us.

We get out of the shower, and Finley lets me borrow a T-shirt and a pair of shorts that almost come down to my knees. I'm almost asleep by the time he shows me into his bedroom.

It's clean, with no sign of the ghosts from the library. I didn't think they'd follow us back here, but then—who knows what to expect after you've been with three ghosts and a man? Anything could happen, and I'd have to take it in stride. I'm too tired to do anything else.

Finley tucks me into bed, then climbs in beside me. The bed creaks with his weight.

The white light in the room gets my attention.

More ghosts?

"The moon is really bright," I tell Finley, then close my eyes. He pulls me close to his side and I lay my head on his chest. "When did it stop raining?"

"I don't know." He runs his hand over my hair. "Guess I wasn't keeping track of the rain."

"What are you thinking about?" I ask with a simper, teasingly. I want to know, even if I'm going to be dreaming in a matter of minutes.

He chuckles at first. "How strong everything felt tonight," he answers right away. "How quickly it all happened."

My eyes open and a guilt washes through me. "Like a spell?" I ask.

"A spell cast by somebody with powerful intentions," he answers.

My face gets hot. "That...might have been me."

"Might have been?" he questions, this time it's him who's teasing.

"It was me," I admit. "I've been... I've been into you for a long time. And after today, I just had to know if you had feelings for me. I didn't..." I explain. "I didn't try to choose for you. I just wanted to know if we were...compatible." Nervousness prickles my skin. I'm glad I told him the truth, but I don't know how he'll react. He doesn't leave me waiting long.

"There's no other woman in the world I'd want to fuck along with three ghosts." Relief washes through me and then I'm met with more surprise. "And I felt that way before today."

"You did?" The shock is clear in my tone.

"Yeah. I did," he admits.

"I...think I'm in love with you," I confess.

"You think?" he questions, peering down at me.

"Maybe I know but I'm scared."

He drops his head to mine as he smiles and runs the tip his nose slightly over mine. "After tonight I don't think you should be afraid of anything."

A nervous huff of a laugh escapes me before he says, "I know I love you."

I can't help but to kiss him. To capture his lips as he brings me closer to his body under the covers.

"I love you," I whisper, my eyes closed and his lips so close.

"I know you do and I love you too," he says and the last thing I feel before drifting to sleep is his smile against my lips.

The End

Looking for more spicy, witchy romance? Snag yourself a copy of The Witch's Fate, and find out what happens when reclusive moon witch Idalis, meets cursed werewolf, Ryker! Keep reading for a sneak peek!

*Idalis*

All I could find in the grimoire was that a storm of this magnitude comes when a soul attempts to evade fate. The knowledge clings to me and yet I cannot make sense of it. Surely, there must be something else. Or someone else who has brought this on.

Secure in my cottage, I close my eyes and listen to the sound of the rain. It's a meditation of sorts. It calms my frayed nerves and gives me a sense of control. At first, I try to pick out individual drops on the roof, then think about the pattern of the down-pour, then concentrate instead on the inside of the cottage. I whisper for it to tell me its secrets. I'm only met with the pounding of the rain and its anger. So I wait, listening and waiting and contemplating if I may have missed something. There must be some-thing...or someone that I have yet to discover.

My cottage is clean and warm and snug. I'm safe inside, and even safer because of the storm.

I am safe.

I breathe in deeply and out even slower, concen-trating on the safety I've built instead of the loneli-ness of it. If my coven still existed, we'd be settled in for the storm by now. The rain is still much too loud for any real conversation, but there are other ways to communicate. We could have written notes, or sat next to each other and worked on spells, or sewed, or cooked. My elder sister would have harnessed the anger of the storm by collecting its water and at that thought, I nearly run for a jar to set it outside but I hesitate. Something inside of me screams not to open the door. My intuition makes me pause.

For a while, I lose myself in memories. I can't remember another storm as strong and sudden as this one, but it's not as if the weather was always sunny and mild. There was the snowstorm that kept us inside for a week straight, with bitter winds and drifts coming halfway up the door. There was the spring freeze that turned the air so cold it hurt to breathe. It was years and years ago. But I remember how I felt...at peace.

We'd *all* danced in a circle in the field, the wind in our hair, until the moons came up. Grateful for the change and the cycles.

Oh—I have so *many* happy memories. They all reassure the same: the storm will be over soon. In this world nothing lasts but everything moves on.

I tell myself that time passes slowly because I'm waiting for it to pass. I keep listening for the rain to let up.

The rain on the roof doesn't soften. It doesn't get quieter. I open my eyes and stare up at the ceiling. It's hard to see with so little light. The only real brightness comes from flashes of lightning. Black clouds at this time of the afternoon just can't last. It is past midday now, though I can't tell exactly how long it's been. With a snap, I light the candles along the windowsill, and ten or so tea lights brighten the space. The flames are small but dignified and useful.

I pass time with a meal of seasoned bread and soft cheeses and delicious jams, then I pay a lot of attention to the steps of brewing a fresh pot of tea. It's chamomile, to calm my nerves. The spoon stirs itself as I watch the ripple of the motion in the teacup. It really does not take long to fiddle with the blend and boil the water and watch it steep, but I drag out as many of the steps as I can, then sip a cup of tea as slowly as I would if it was part of a ritual.

The storm *still* does not let up. The irritation and unsettled feelings it brings are unwelcome.

My heart beats faster at the idea that it might never let up, and the field might slowly fill with water and cover the cottage.

*That* will not happen, I promise myself sternly. There is too much earth around me. It will absorb the rain, and more flowers will bloom if the sun comes out.

*When* the sun comes back out. And *when* the sun comes back out, I will take my reply to Prince Adom and Princess Charlotte to the letter box along with the gift, and soon all will be well.

I trace the path to the royal palace in my mind, wandering over the path through the woods, which I know very well; over roads I know less well; and finally through the city that surrounds the palace. I picture booths on the market streets where I once stopped to haggle over items with the rest of the coven. I picture pubs and inns and shops decorated for the royal wedding. I picture a bustling city with guests from all over the world gathering ahead of the ceremony and passing the time with dancing and games and conversation. People will be up at all hours of the night. There will always be someone talking. The excitement will grow until the day of the wedding, and then it will spill into the streets with nothing but joyous celebration.

In the stories they tell afterward, they will have been within arm's reach of Princess Charlotte's gown and close enough to hear the vows she and Prince Adom will speak to each other. Mothers and fathers will tell their children stories of the day for years, and children will fall asleep hoping that one day they'll be able to go to a royal wedding, too.

I get carried away with the vision of it and have to cough to clear my throat. Look at me—a few hours alone in a storm, safe in my cottage, and I'm having all kinds of feelings about a royal wedding that I do not want to attend.

Perhaps I should lie down and go to bed for the

night. It must be toward evening. It is earlier than usual, that is true, but it is so dark that the time does not matter much.

If the storm isn't going to let up, then the sound could send me to sleep. It's not so different from the sea.

I have just committed to the idea when there is a knock at the door.

My body freezes, my legs as stiff as stone. I'm in a half-crouch, stuck between sitting and standing, and my thoughts are filled with the rain. Surely, I did not hear a knock. Surely, it was the rain or the wind— some element of the storm. A piece of earth blown across the hills and slapped wetly on the door.

But that knock—that imagined knock, I only thought it was a knock—did not sound wet, like a piece of earth. My heart bucks and a fear I recognize all too well comes over me.

I do not move, other than my pounding heart. It was nothing. It was nothing, and I have nothing to fear.

Another knock comes.

This one is undeniable. Despite the rain, so loud on the roof that I can hardly hear my own breathing, and despite the wind, which howls past the cottage, that is unmistakably someone's fist pounding at the door. My throat dries and tightens. Did I not cast the spell to not be seen?

I imagine the size of the fist it would take to make that sound, audible over the rain, and the strength someone would need to possess. Even to reach the cottage in the first place cannot have been easy.

Dread fills me, chilling me from head to toe. I wave a hand at the shutters out of an old habit, but they are firmly shut and latched so tight that even my panicked magic does not budge them.

Whoever is outside cannot get in...unless they have the strength to break down the door or punch through my protection spells and the walls itself.

More questions flood my mind, carrying on the wave of my dread. Who would come here in the middle of a terrible storm? Who in all the lands would think to knock on *my* door? I know the rumors that are said about me in every village I have ever visited, because I have had a hand in starting those rumors. On the few occasions that I've left the cottage and spent time in cities and villages since I lost my coven, I have made a point of asking a quiet question or two to someone in a tavern who looks like they are fond of travel.

I do not exaggerate much. I am true to the extent of my powers, which are considerable in comparison to someone who cannot wield magic. I am also true to my desire to be left alone.

*I have heard there is a witch in Athica who lives by herself,* I will say, keeping my voice low and checking over my shoulder as if I expect to be overheard. *I have heard she is powerful and angry. Have you heard of this witch? She requires many miles of space around her cottage or else...* I let the person I am talking to fill in the blank of what *or else* might mean.

Gossip is a tried and true way to put information into the world. Travelers need some form of payment for their presence at an inn, and a neat piece of gossip is a way to form quick bonds with other people. I know these travelers.

And yet someone is here. In all the years no one has dared. Perhaps they know not where they are or who I am. A lost wanderer in the storm. Empathy overwhelms me but still I am wise to keep my guard up.

Cautiously, I finish standing up, shaking myself out of my frozen, indecisive state.

It is only a few steps to the kitchen, where the athame hangs from a hook, cradled in a leather sheath. I swing the sheath over my head and pull it into place on my shoulder, then draw the athame.

I am more grounded the moment my fingers close around the silver hilt. The blade is sharp and well-maintained, and I have practiced with it for years.

A deep exhale steadies me as I wave a hand at the grate. A roaring fire springs up, filling the cottage with flickering orange light. The flames leap higher and higher, throwing heat out of the grate as well, and the power settles me even more.

There. Armed with a blade and with my powers, I face the door as a third knock forces the wooden door to tremble.

With a few deep breaths, I approach the door, leaving a foot or two of space between myself and the thick wood. On the other side is a stranger.

Still, I wait for a few more seconds, half of me praying that this strange visitor will disappear back into the rain and half of me praying that they will knock again. It is such an odd sensation that I feel almost dizzy with it. Or is that another shift in the magic? I cannot tell. A person at my door is *so* out of the ordinary that I can do nothing but face each second as it comes.

"Who goes there?" I call out. My voice does not

waver. Strength finds me even still. I imagine my coven at my back, waiting with their chins held high, armed with their own powers and their faith in me.

That is always how they were. That is why they decided to go and fight in the war.

"I am alone," a voice says through the door, rumbling and gruff. Strong, even through solid wood. "And my portal has failed me. My commander"—a peal of thunder drowns out a few words—"come to you. He said you may be able to help." My first reaction is one of shock. I am stunned. There is a man outside my door. With a voice that brings a certain feeling to the depths of me that I haven't felt in so long.

I push aside the delicious sound of the being's voice and focus on his words.

"Your commander?" I question. What reason would a commander have for sending a soldier here? To *my* lands, where I am the only person for miles? What business would an army have? "Why are you here?" The thinly veiled anger is deliberate. "This is my property," I call out.

"I came to collect flowers for a wedding," he says, his voice seeming carefully tense. I wish I could hear him better, but I would have to open the door to do that, and I will *not* be reckless about opening the door. Instead I stare at the intricately carved doorknob. The metal holds a spell within it. *No one shall pass who wishes me harm.* I remind myself of that spell as I soak in the stranger's tale.

Flowers for a wedding? Who sends a soldier to collect flowers for a wedding?

"Show them to me," I tell him. "Bring them to the window." I'm lifting my hand to open a pair of the shutters when he makes a sound.

"I sent them through my portal before it failed. I don't have them any longer."

A sarcastic laugh leaves me. How utterly ridiculous a lie. "Then how can I trust you?"

There is another long pause. My heart flutters, and it is not the flutter that warns me of danger. It is the flutter of curiosity. Who is this man? And what has truly brought him?

I shake my head, trying to get rid of that feeling. Curiosity brings danger. It can make a person forget to protect themselves.

The curiosity I feel won't leave me alone. More questions come to mind. What if it was this soldier who changed the magic in the land? What if *he* was the one who summoned the storm? There's another shift around me and it's then I hear the crack of thunder far too close.

"I am at a loss—" He raises his voice and then pauses again to let another loud crash of thunder die down. "I do not wish to disturb you," the soldier says, starting again. "But with the rain and the lack of a portal, I am trapped." The smallest break in his voice speaks of his honesty. "And I am at your mercy."

I cannot speak.

I search for the words to reply, but I can't think of what to say.

"I ask," he continues, "that you take pity on me. I will not stay long. Only as long as it takes for my portal to charge. Then I will go and leave you in peace."

It is not the first time a being has been at my mercy. Many beings who cannot cast spells but need one to get by have been at my mercy. I have received letters from frantic mothers and desperate fathers. I have heard from determined daughters and sons who will not rest until they have a solution. I have received a great many requests for mercy in the words that pour off the pages in my letter box.

My heart aches with empathy as if I'm the one who's cut off from home. Yes, I have lived in the cottage alone for the years since my coven was taken. I kept our physical home, but not the people who *made* it home, and I have been homesick for them more often than I haven't.

I know what it is to be far from everything you know without a way to get back.

I wave my hand at the door, undoing the latch and the bolts, then pull it open fast, before I can lose my nerve. If he can step through the doorway, he may enter. It is as simple as that. I will aid him in leaving this place as soon as the storm passes.

Outside, it is very dark from the thunderclouds, but more lightning burns across the sky, and there he is.

Something shifts wildly when I open the door. My heart won't behave, and my lungs don't know what to do. The sight of him...it does something to me I've never felt before.

He is tall and broad and muscled, wearing leather armor. Every inch of him that I can see is soaked from the rain, and dark hair runs in streaks across his forehead. He does not look like the kind of man who would ever need someone's pity. Certainly not mine. He is too strong. His presence overwhelms me. The shadows from my fire cast shadows on his sharp features, and it is like a gust of wind has come into the house and stolen my breath all over again.

My curiosity is no less powerful. It feels like a fire raging through me.

This soldier is the most gorgeous man I have ever seen.

A Spell Jar for Courage

RECIPE REQUIREMENTS:

A jar with a cork lid to carry the spell

A pinch of salt to cleanse and purify

Tiger's eye crystal for courage

A sprinkle of cinnamon (or a stick of bark) for abundance

Orange candle to seal the jar

Add your ingredients one at a time, stating the intention and purpose of each ingredient as you touch it. As the wax seals the jar, state the following:

*For the good of all and to the harm of none, I am my own hero. Within me I possess the courage to open every door. I am able to walk through any space I desire. I am guided, protected, and being shown all possibilities for my higher self with strength. There is nothing that can stop me for I am capable and worthy. Courage walks beside me and holds my hand when I am in need.*

When the wax has covered the lid and sealed the spell in the jar, blow out the candle and whisper, "So mote it be." Keep the jar in a safe place and shake if necessary to remind yourself of this truth: you already possess all the courage you will ever need.

Scan the QR code below to get your copy of
The Witch's Fate

# ABOUT WILLOW WINTERS

Thank you so much for reading my romances. I'm just a stay at home mom and avid reader turned author and I couldn't be happier.

I hope you love my books as much as I do!

To browse more of my books, visit willowwinterswrites.com/pages/reading-order

or scan

**Valetti Crime Family Series:**
A HOT mafia series to sink your teeth into.

Dirty Dom
Becca came to pay off a debt, but **Dominic Valetti** wanted more.
So he did what he's always done, and took what he wanted.

His Hostage
Elle finds herself in the wrong place at the wrong time. The mafia doesn't let witnesses simply walk away.
Regret has a name, and it's **Vincent Valetti.**

Rough Touch

Ava is looking for revenge at any cost so long as she can remember the girl she used to be.

But she doesn't expect **Kane** to show up and show her kindness that will break her.

Cuffed Kiss

**Tommy Valetti** is a thug, a mistake, and everything Tonya needs; the answers to numb the pain of her past.

Depraved Lust (formerly Bad Boy)

**Anthony** is the hitman for the Valetti familia, and damn good at what he does. They want men to talk, he makes them talk. They want men gone, bang - it's done. It's as simple as that.

Until Catherine.

Those Boys Are Trouble (Valetti Crime Family Collection)

**Sexy, thrilling with a touch of dark Standalone Novels**

**Broken (Standalone)**

**Kade** is ruthless and cold hearted in the criminal world.

They gave Olivia to him. To break. To do as he'd like. All because she was in the wrong place at the wrong time.  But there are secrets that change everything. And once he has her, he's never letting her go.

Forsaken, (A Dark Romance cowritten with B. B. Hamel)

Grace is stolen and gifted to him; Geo a dominating, brutal and a cold hearted killer.

However, with each gentle touch and act of kindness that lures her closer to him, Grace is finding it impossible to remember why she should fight him.

**Highest Bidder Series:**

Bought

Sold

Owned

Given

From USA Today best selling authors, Willow Winters and Lauren Landish, comes a sexy and forbidden series of standalone romances.

Highest Bidder Collection (All four Highest Bidder Novels)

**Bad Boy Standalones, cowritten with Lauren Landish:**

Inked

Tempted

Mr. CEO

Three novels featuring sexy powerful heroes.
Three romances that are just as swoon-worthy as they are tempting.

Simply Irresistible (A Bad Boy Collection)

**Contemporary Romance Standalones**

**Knocking Boots (A Novel)**
They were never meant to be together.
**Charlie** is a bartender with noncommittal tendencies.
Grace is looking for the opposite. Commitment. Marriage. A baby.

**Promise Me (A Novel)**
She gave him her heart. Back when she thought

they'd always be together.

Now **Hunter** is home and he wants Violet back.

**Tell Me To Stay (A Novella)**

He devoured her, and she did the same to him.

Until it all fell apart and Sophie ran as far away from

**Madox** as she could.

After all, the two of them were never meant to be

together?

**Second Chance (A Novella)**

No one knows what happened the night that forced

them apart. No one can ever know.

But the moment **Nathan** locks his light blue eyes on

Harlow again, she is ruined.

She never stood a chance.

**Burned Promises (A Novella)**

**Derek** made her a promise. And then he broke it.

That's what happens with your first love.

But Emma didn't expect for Derek to fall back into

her life and for her to fall back into his bed.

**Small Town Romance**

Tequila Rose Book 1

Autumn Night Whiskey Book 2
He tasted like tequila and the fake name I gave him was Rose.
Four years ago, I decided to get over one man, by getting under another. A single night and nothing more.
Now, with a three-year-old in tow, the man I still dream about is staring at me from across the street in the town I grew up in. I don't miss the flash of recognition, or the heat in his gaze.
The chemistry is still there, even after all these years.
I just hope the secrets and regrets don't destroy our second chance before it's even begun.

**Tequila Rose World Standalones**

A Little Bit Dirty

Kiss Me in this Small Town

**You Are Mine Series of Duets**

You Are My Reason (You Are Mine Duet book 1)
You Are My Hope (You Are Mine Duet book 2)

**Mason** and Jules emotionally gripping romantic suspense duet.
One look and Jules was tempted; one taste, addicted.
No one is perfect, but that's how it felt to be in Mason's arms.
But will the sins of his past tear them apart?

You Know I Love You
You Know I Need You
Kat says goodbye to the one man she ever loved even though **Evan** begs her to trust him.
With secrets she couldn't have possibly imagined, Kat is torn between what's right and what was right for them.

Tell Me You Want Me
This is Sue's story.

**Forget Me Not  (Standalone novel)**
She loved a boy a long time ago.  He helped her escape and she left him behind.  Regret followed her every day after.
**Jay,** the boy she used to know, came back, a man.  With a grip strong enough to keep her close and a look in his eyes that warned her to never dare leave him again.

It's dark and twisted.
But that doesn't make it any less of what it is.
A love story. Our love story.

**It's Our Secret (Standalone novel)**
It was only a little lie. That's how stories like these
get started.
But with every lie Allison tells, **Dean** sees through it.
She didn't know what would happen. But with all
the secrets and lies, she never thought she'd fall for
him.

*Read Willow's sexiest and most talked about romances in
the Merciless World*

**A Kiss to Tell (a standalone novel)**
They lived on the same street and went to the same
school, although he was a year ahead. Even so close,
he was untouchable.
**Sebastian** was bad news and Chloe was the sad girl
who didn't belong.
Then one night changed everything.

**Possessive (a standalone novel)**
It was never love with **Daniel Cross** and she never

thought it would be. It was only lust from a distance. Unrequited love maybe.

He's a man Addison could never have, for so many reasons.

**Merciless Saga**
Merciless
Heartless
Breathless
Endless

Ruthless, crime family leader **Carter Cross** should've known Aria would ruin him the moment he saw her. Given to Carter to start a war; he was too eager to accept. But what he didn't know was what Aria would do to him. He didn't know that she would change everything.

All He'll Ever Be (Merciless Series Collection of all 4 novels)

**Irresistible Attraction Trilogy**
A Single Glance
A Single Kiss
A Single Touch

Bethany is looking for answers and to find them she needs one of the brothers of an infamous crime family, **Jase Cross.**
Even a sizzling love affair won't stop her from getting what she needs.
But Bethany soon comes to realise Jase will be her downfall, and she's determined to be his just the same.

Irresistible Attraction (A Single Glance Trilogy Collection)

**Hard to Love Series**
Hard to Love
Desperate to Touch
Tempted to Kiss
Easy to Fall

Eight years ago she ran from him.
Laura should have known he'd come for her. Men like **Seth King** always get what they want.
Laura knows what Seth wants from her, and she knows it comes with a steep price.
However it's a risk both of them will take.

Not My Heart to Break (Hard to Love Series Collection)

**This Love Hurts Trilogy**
This Love Hurts
But I Need You
And I Love You the Most

An epic tale of both betrayal and all-consuming love...
**Marcus,** the villain.
**Cody Walsh,** the FBI agent who knows too much.
And Delilah, the lawyer caught in between.

What I Would do for You (This Love Hurts Trilogy Collection)

**Shame On You Series**
Tease Me Once
I'll Kiss You Twice
Then You're Mine
Tease me once... I'll kiss you twice.
**Declan Cross'** story from the Merciless World.

**Spin off of the Merciless World**

Love the Way Trilogy
Kiss Me
Hold Me
Love Me

With everything I've been through, and the unfortunate way we met, the last thing I thought I'd be focused on is the fact that I love the way you kiss me.

**Extended epilogues to the Merciless World Novels**
A Kiss To Keep (more of Sebastian and Chloe)
Seductive (more of Daniel and Addison)
Effortless (more of Carter and Aria)
Never to End (more of Seth and Laura)

**To Be Claimed Saga**
A hot tempting series of fated love, lust-filled secrets and the beginnings of an epic war.

Wounded Kiss
Gentle Scars
Primal Lust
Broken Fate
Captive Desire
Under His Reign

## Collections of shorts and novellas

Don't Let Go
A collection of stories including:
Infatuation
Desires in the Night and Keeping Secrets
Bad Boy Next Door

Kisses and Wishes
A collection of holiday stories including:
One Holiday Wish
Collared for Christmas
Stolen Mistletoe Kisses

All I Want is a Kiss (A Holiday short)
Olivia thought fleeting weekends would be enough
and it always was, until the distance threatened to
tear her and **Nicholas** apart for good.

www.ingramcontent.com/pod-product-compliance
Lightning Source LLC
Chambersburg PA
CBHW030008010826
48973CB00009B/2711